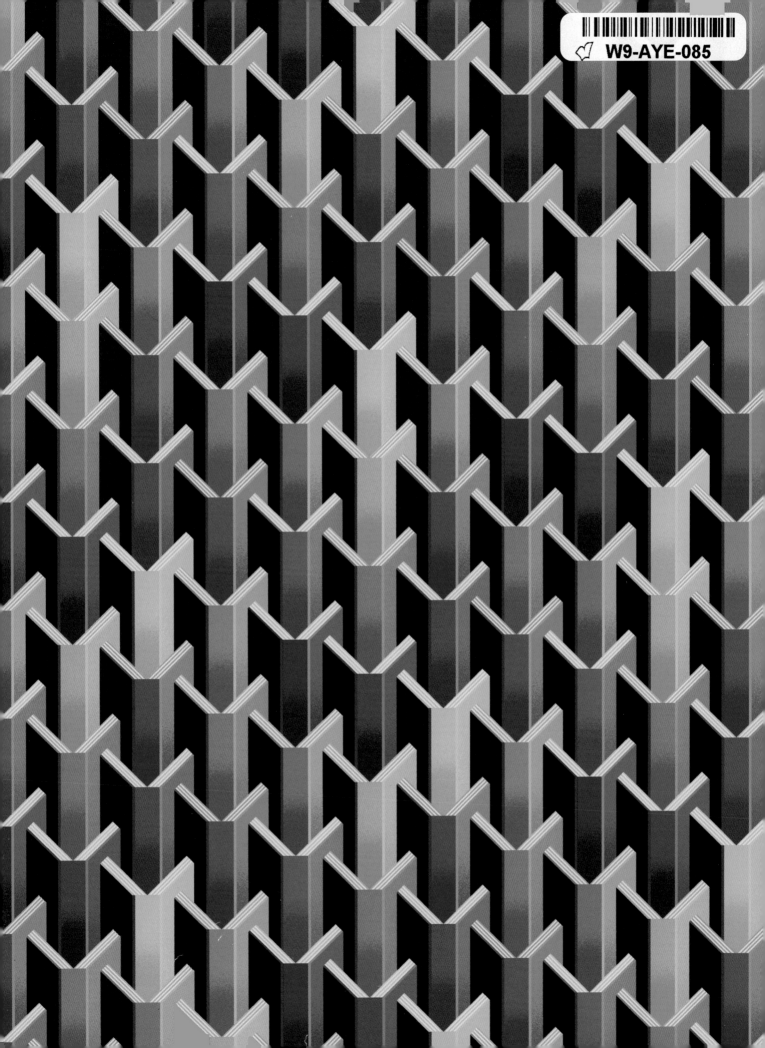

For every librarian who, through Patience and Fortitude,
guides a child to discover their own book of gold

Copyright © 2017 by Bob Staake
All rights reserved. Published in the United States by Schwartz & Wade Books,
an imprint of Random House Children's Books, a division of Penguin Random House LLC, New York.
Schwartz & Wade Books and the colophon are trademarks of Penguin Random House LLC.

Visit us on the Web! randomhousekids.com
Educators and librarians, for a variety of teaching tools, visit us at RHTeachersLibrarians.com

Library of Congress Cataloging-in-Publication Data
Names: Staake, Bob, author, illustrator.
Title: The Book of Gold / Bob Staake.
Description: First edition. | New York: Schwartz & Wade Books, [2017] | Summary: "Isaac isn't interested in much, but when a mysterious shopkeeper tells him about a legendary book that holds the answers to every question ever asked, he embarks on a lifelong search for the Book of Gold" –Provided by publisher.
Identifiers: LCCN 2016000770 (print) | LCCN 2016025493 (ebook) | ISBN 978-0-553-51077-5 (hc)
ISBN 978-0-553-51078-2 (glb) | ISBN 978-0-553-51079-9 (ebk)
Subjects: | CYAC: Books and reading–Fiction. | Questions and answers–Fiction.
Classification: LCC PZ7.S77439 Bo 2017 (print) | LCC PZ7.S77439 (ebook) | DDC [E]–dc23

The text of this book is set in Brandon Grotesque.

The illustrations were rendered digitally.

MANUFACTURED IN CHINA
2 4 6 8 10 9 7 5 3 1
First Edition

The
Book
Of
Gold

BOB STAAKE

schwartz & wade books · new york

Isaac Gutenberg wasn't interested in much. Not in toys, not in the funny papers, not even in his pet goldfish.

His parents tried to tempt him with books.

"How about I read you a story about a dinosaur, dear?" asked his mother.

"Dinosaurs are LONG gone," huffed Isaac.

"My goodness, Isaac. Look at how tall this skyscraper is," said his father, pointing to a page.

"Skyscrapers are ALWAYS tall," replied Isaac.

It was a beautiful spring day in 1935 when Isaac's parents took him on the trolley over the East River from Brooklyn into New York City.

"Oh, how I love those lions!" Isaac's father exclaimed as they made their way up the steps of the New York Public Library.

"Aren't they amazing, Isaac?" asked his mother. "They're busy guarding the thousands and thousands of books inside."

"An entire building filled with books?" Isaac groaned. "Do we *have* to go in?"

Isaac's parents loved books. They adored how they smelled and the way they felt in their hands, but most of all, they loved discovering the answers hidden inside.

"Isaac, have you ever wondered how wide a single eye on the Statue of Liberty is?" asked his mother as she leafed through a book.

Isaac sulked. "Does it matter?" he asked.

"Isaac, did you know that men with giant earth movers built a canal in Panama to create a shortcut between the Atlantic and Pacific Oceans?" asked his father.

But Isaac had his own question: "Can we go home yet?"

As the Gutenbergs left the library and strolled along Forty-Second Street, Isaac's mother glanced in a store window.

"Ah," she said, "this shop might have the perfect birthday gift for your aunt Sadie!"

Isaac sighed.

It was a strange store filled floor to ceiling with curious things. There was an elephant head hanging on a wall, and a suit of armor. There was even a dinosaur bone displayed beneath a fancy glass dome.

While his father and mother looked at the dusty knickknacks, Isaac sat down on the cold tile floor and waited.

"You're not interested in the tin toys, young man?" asked the old shopkeeper as she stepped closer.

"Not really," he said.

"Then how about a steam locomotive?" she asked.

"Nope," sighed Isaac.

The shopkeeper froze. Her violet eyes grew wider.

"Tell me, child," she whispered. "Have you heard about *The Book of Gold*?"

Isaac shook his head.

"There is a legend," she explained, "that somewhere in the world there is one very special book that's just waiting to be discovered. It will look like any other book, but it holds all the answers to every question ever asked, and when it is opened, it turns to *solid gold*."

"A book that turns into gold?" asked Isaac. He couldn't imagine anything greater—he'd be rich! "You mean I could be the one to find that book?"

"Of course you could!" The shopkeeper smiled knowingly.

As the Gutenbergs left with Aunt Sadie's gift, the old shopkeeper called out to Isaac, "Good luck in your search, young man. You'll need patience and fortitude to find *The Book of Gold*!"

But Isaac didn't hear her—he was already out the door.

Isaac ran into the first bookstore he could find. He opened a book about pirates, but nothing happened. He opened many other books, then slammed them closed.

Isaac peeked into the window of a diner and saw a book on the counter. He ran in and opened it, but the book didn't turn to gold.

He noticed a book fall from a woman's purse. He picked it up and excitedly opened it, but again nothing happened.

On the trip home, he spied a book left on

a trolley seat. He opened it, but this book didn't turn to gold either.

Isaac flew up the stairs of his apartment and went straight to a cabinet filled with books. He opened one after another as fast as he could—and dropped them even faster into a big pile.

For days and months, Isaac continued to search. It was more difficult than he had ever imagined. As hard as he tried, he could not find *The Book of Gold,* but one day something quite unexpected happened.

Isaac opened a book called *The Seven Wonders of the World*, and a question popped into his head:

Why don't the pyramids have windows?

That was the first of many questions.

With every new book he opened, Isaac grew more curious.

How can something as heavy as a ship float?

Who invented pizza?

Were dinosaurs ever covered in fur?

By the time he was ten years old, Isaac's questions became even more profound.

How did the number eight get its name?

If gravity didn't exist, could you still fly a kite?

Why don't elevators also travel sideways?

Isaac grew up.

He became a teenager,

and then a man,

and he never forgot what the old shopkeeper had told him about *The Book of Gold* all those years before.

Isaac searched, and searched, and searched some more—and in the back of his mind, he worried that someone else might discover the book before he did.

He scoured libraries for old books, and bookstores for new ones. He climbed into the dark attics of friends to pick through their musty boxes. He visited flea markets and yard sales and junk shops.

As the years went by, Isaac picked up fewer books—because he found himself reading every one he opened.

Isaac was *discovering*.

He learned who invented pizza. He saw diagrams showing how heavy ships could float. He had yet to discover how the number eight got its name, but he was sure he'd eventually find the answer.

Still he kept searching.

As he read more and more, Isaac's world grew bigger— and soon he found himself traveling great distances.

One summer, he took a plane to India on a hunch that he might find *The Book of Gold* in a street bazaar in Calcutta.

Another year he traveled to Russia to see if the book might be hidden in one of the onion-shaped domes of the towers overlooking Red Square.

Twice he sailed by ship to Egypt because he believed *The Book of Gold* might very well be buried in a pharaoh's tomb. Isaac didn't find the elusive book, but he finally learned why the pyramids had been built without windows.

Isaac was old now, a man of eighty.

He walked slowly, and his eyesight was beginning to fail.

Though the rickety trolley he had often ridden as a boy was long gone,

he could still travel from Brooklyn into New York City by subway.
When Isaac strolled through the city, he couldn't believe how much

The lion on the left was named Patience, and the one on the right was Fortitude.

"Ahhhh," sighed Isaac.

He sank into a comfy chair to rest his weary legs. His thoughts wandered back to the first time he had visited the library. He reflected on his mother and father and he remembered the mysterious old shopkeeper.

He now realized that he probably would never find *The Book of Gold,* but because of that book, Isaac had asked questions and searched for answers. He had visited distant lands, and had used his imagination to go to places he'd never been. He had lived a long life filled with wonder.

Isaac looked around the library. He saw a girl in her mother's lap looking at pictures in a book. He watched a young man reach high to pull down a book about robots. He saw people leafing through pages and others reading in big, cozy chairs.

They were all searching.

Then Isaac noticed a little boy. He was sitting at the same table piled with books where Isaac had sat so many years ago.

The library began to glow like the sun itself, a golden aura encircling them.

Isaac stood up, steadied himself with his cane, and slowly approached the boy.

Isaac's eyes grew wider.

"Tell me, child," he whispered. "Have *you* heard about *The Book of Gold*?"